Laura

By Binette Schroeder

Translated by
Rosemary Lanning

NORTH-SOUTH BOOKS
New York / London

Aunt Ann Tan was still fast
asleep. Laura looked out of
the window. Far away among
the trees something
shimmered mysteriously.
What could it be? she
wondered. She quickly
slipped on her clothes; tucked
her bear Bobo under her arm;
and ran across the misty
meadows to the forest.

The forest was cool and still.
Laura came to a clearing
where she found a nest.
In the nest lay an
egg with a big, long nose.

"Oh," whispered Laura,
"it's a real Humpty Dumpty!"

"Ugh!" cried the egg.
"It's a real human!"
He leapt out of the nest and
ran off into the deep dark forest.
Laura ran after him.

"Good morning,"
said Humpty Dumpty,
looking sideways at Laura.
"What's your name?"
"I'm Laura," said Laura.
Then Humpty Dumpty sang:
"Laura-la, Laura-lee,
Do you want to play with me?"

And they played
cloud dancing
water falling
tree throwing
rock wobbling
beetle waking
snail teasing
flower ruffling
leaf sliding
until they
were quite
out of breath.

Then evening came.

"What a shame," said Laura. "I have to
go now."

"So soon?" asked Humpty Dumpty
with a catch in his voice.

"Are you afraid of the dark?" asked Laura.
Humpty Dumpty gulped.
"At night the thundersmasher birds come, and
I'm all alone. They are wild and dangerous
and hungry . . . and eggs are what they most like
to eat."
"I'll tell you what," said Laura. "I'll leave Bobo
with you. Then you won't need to be afraid."
And she put the bear into his arms and headed
for home.

During the night there was terrible thunder and
lightning. The tree house swung and swayed
in the storm. Aunt Ann Tan was sound asleep.
"It's the thundersmasher birds!" cried Laura.
She jumped out of her hammock, hurried out
of the house and down the shaking staircase,
and raced out into the stormy night, calling . . .

Humpty Dumpty, I'M COMING!

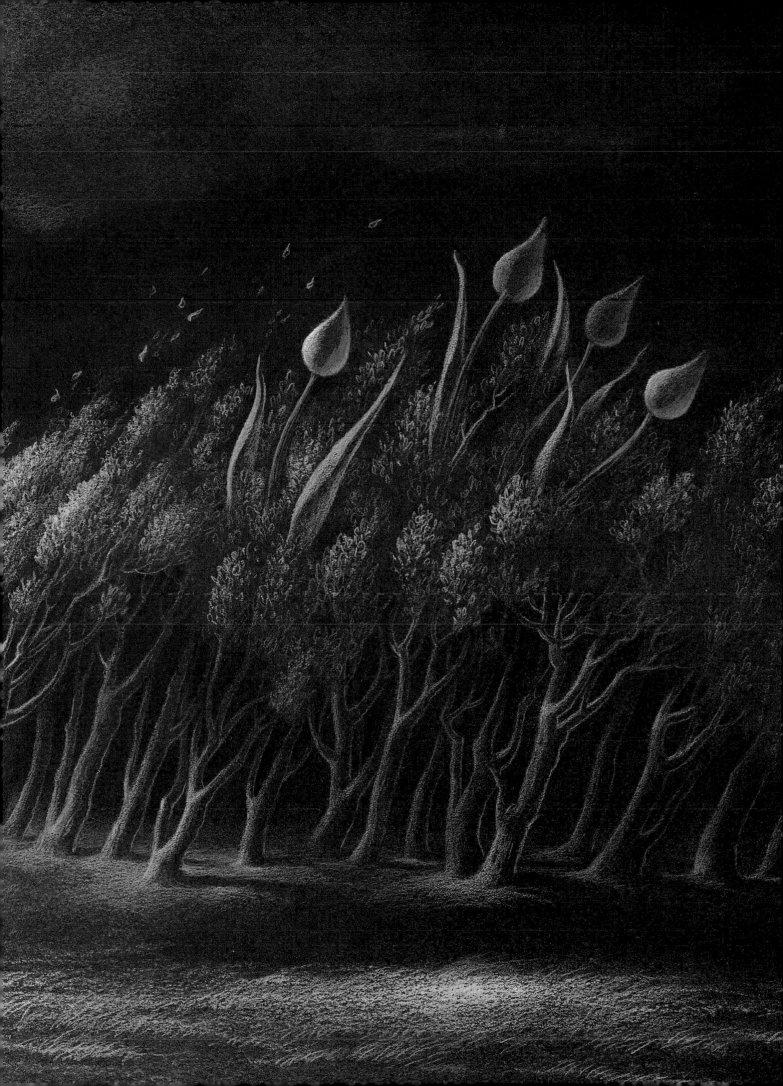

Suddenly
it was still.
The moon shone
and all was well.

Morning came.
Laura squinted
sleepily into
the sun.
"Humpty Dumpty,
are you there?
Where are you?
Humpty Dumpty!
Humpty Dumpty!"

Then she saw the
eggshell on the ground.
"It was the thundersmasher
birds!" she said,
and her voice trembled.
Then she cried
and cried
and cried.

Suddenly a voice beside
her said:

GOOD MORNING, LAURA. Shall we play again?

Copyright © 1999 by Nord-Süd Verlag AG, Gossau Zürich, Switzerland
First published in Switzerland under the title Laura
English translation copyright © 1999 by North-South Books Inc.

All rights reserved.

First published in the United States, Great Britain, Canada,
Australia, and New Zealand in 1999 by North-South Books,
an imprint of Nord-Süd Verlag AG, Gossau Zürich, Switzerland.

Distributed in the United States by North-South Books Inc.,
New York.

Library of Congress Cataloging-in-Publication Data is available.
A CIP catalogue record for this book is available from
The British Library.

ISBN 0-7358-1170-9 (trade binding)
TB 10 9 8 7 6 5 4 3 2 1
ISBN 0-7358-1171-7 (library binding)
LB 10 9 8 7 6 5 4 3 2 1

Printed in Italy